The Tale of the Troublesome Toad

Written by Quentin Flynn
Illustrated by Richard Hoit

Contents

NELSON
A Cengage Company

Meet the Characters

Monsieur la Verrue

A rather vain toad.

Monsieur Cheval

A simple farm horse.

Mademoiselle Jument

A stylish horse.

Monsieur Lapin

The village baker.

Mademoiselle du Merle

A young bluebird.

Madame Minette

A cat.

Monsieur le Canard

A well-dressed duck.

POST CARD

Dear Reader

Sometimes, your friends may tell you how you should look, behave or do things. They're only trying to be helpful, but sometimes it's better just to be yourself. After all, if they are true friends, they will like you for who you are, not who you could be. Here's a fable about why you should not always listen to well-meaning advice!

Quentin Flynn
Author

The Village Square

1. Monsieur Cheval's barn
2. Lapin et fils bakery
3. The Beauchamp bus stop

1 A Magnificent Toad

Monsieur la Verrue was standing on an old suitcase on the banks of a pond. He gazed at his reflection in the glassy pond.

He checked that all his magnificent warts were still in place. His slimy grey lips curled into a toady grin and he winked at himself with a giant bulging eye. Then he blew up his throat and let out a loud burp.

“Rrraarp! Ah, that feels better!” he said. He looked around to check no one had heard him. “Starting the morning with a bowl brimming with slug-o-pops always makes me burp.”

He stared back into the water. Satisfied that he could not be a more handsome toad, he clambered off his suitcase.

Monsieur la Verrue peered up at the sun, which had risen just above the treetops. Resisting one last admiring glance at himself, he grasped the handle of the suitcase. He headed for the bus stop.

"A week's holiday in Beauchamp," he croaked to himself. He leaned nonchalantly against the sign that said "Arrêt d'autobus".

"Oh, I am looking forward to getting on the bus."

"Rrraarp!"

Monsieur la Verrue cast his eyes upwards. "Someone should change those wooden signs to metal ones," he thought to himself. "One simply cannot see one's reflection in a wooden sign!"

Resigned to not preening himself in the reflection of the sign, Monsieur la Verrue practised his nonchalant pose. Then he tried a nonchalant and haughty pose, which involved lowering his eyelids until his eyes were just slits. Then he tried a nonchalant and disdainful pose, which involved curling the corners of his lips downwards. He was about to try a nonchalant and imperious pose, which involved raising his nostrils skywards, when he was interrupted by the sound of a loud *toot* and a bus door swishing open.

"Oops, sorry!" called the bus driver. "I didn't mean to catch you in the middle of ... of ... Didn't your mother tell you to go before you left the house?"

Monsieur la Verrue spluttered indignantly. He picked up his suitcase and climbed aboard the bus, with a look that he hoped was haughty, disdainful and imperious all at the same time.

He saw an empty seat next to a rather well-groomed and stylish passenger.

"She'll be pleased to have me sitting next to her," he thought with a smile.

"Bonjour, Mademoiselle," he purred as he slid into the spare seat. "My name, in case you did not already know, is Monsieur la Verrue."

"Bonjour, Monsieur la Verrue," she replied. "I am Mademoiselle Jument."

Monsieur la Verrue detected a slight air of unease about Mademoiselle Jument's greeting, but he was used to that. It was not often that ordinary folk got to sit next to a toad as spectacularly magnificent, sophisticated and handsome as he was.

He popped his suitcase under the seat. He settled back with a satisfied “Rrraarp”. He allowed Mademoiselle Jument to bask in his greatness.

“Rrraarp!”

2 A Busy Morning

Monsieur Lapin's bakery, Lapin et fils, was where all the villagers of Beauchamp loved to start their day. The aroma of freshly baked baguettes drifted through the cobblestone streets every morning like an invisible alarm clock.

Monsieur Cheval, Madame Minette, Monsieur le Canard and Mademoiselle du Merle were basking in the sunshine outside Lapin et fils. A few scattered crumbs were all that was left from their breakfast baguettes. Now there was nothing left to do except enjoy the warmth of the sun and each other's company while they waited for lunch.

Monsieur Lapin carried his stool outside to join them.

"What a busy morning," he said.

"Yes, very busy," agreed Monsieur le Canard.

"Very very busy," nodded Madame Minette.

Arrêt d'autobus
Lapin et fils

"Very very very busy," observed Mademoiselle du Merle.

"Have you made any pastries? All this talk of busy-ness is making me hungry," said Monsieur Cheval.

Monsieur Lapin shook his head. "I'm afraid you'll have to wait until my pastry flour is delivered later this morning. I have three sacks being brought to me on the bus."

Three sacks! Monsieur Cheval dreamed about how many pastries that would make. He licked his lips.

"I could wait at the bus stop for you," he said helpfully. "That way, you could focus on getting the rest of the ingredients ready."

"Thank you, Monsieur Cheval," smiled Monsieur Lapin. "That would be a great help."

Monsieur Cheval beamed. He liked being helpful, especially where pastries were concerned. He flicked his ears back, feeling most pleased with himself. And then, after five minutes, a thought crept into his head. His ears flicked forward again.

"Where exactly is the bus stop, Monsieur Lapin?"

Monsieur Lapin chuckled.

"Why, it's right here," he replied, pointing at the sign fixed to the gas lamp outside the bakery.

"Arrêt d'autobus," declared the sign.

"Well, there's a spot of luck," smiled Monsieur Cheval. "I was just checking that you knew that."

"I do," smiled Monsieur Lapin.

"I'll wait here with you," offered Madame Minette, winking at Monsieur Cheval.

"Me too," said Monsieur le Canard.

Mademoiselle du Merle checked her diary.

"Count me in," she said.

"That's settled then," said Monsieur Lapin.

The baker and the rest of the villagers sat with their backs resting against the warm stone bakery, closed their eyes and got on with the very important job they had all volunteered to do.

3 A Vision of Beauty

Monsieur Cheval awoke with a startled look upon his face. What was that noise? He shook his head and stared at the face that had appeared in front of him.

"Rrraarp!"

The noise had abruptly ended the slumbering mid-morning naps that the other villagers were enjoying too, and they all struggled to their feet.

"Rrraarp!" repeated Monsieur la Verrue, who was standing in front of a bus that was purring patiently beneath the "Arrêt d'autobus" sign. At the rear of the bus, Monsieur Lapin was unloading the last of three sacks of pastry flour onto his trolley and waving cheerily to the bus driver.

Beauchamp
Arrêt d'autobus

Monsieur Cheval remembered he had something important to do and called out to Monsieur Lapin. "It's here!" he bellowed helpfully. "The bus is here."

"So it is, Monsieur Cheval," replied Monsieur Lapin as he wheeled the three sacks inside the green door of his bakery. "Thank you. Well done."

Having completed his very important task, Monsieur Cheval was about to turn his attention back to the face in front of him when suddenly he was transfixed by a vision that made his jaw drop, his heart skip a beat, and all thoughts of warm, custardy pastries vanish in an instant.

Alighting from the step of the bus was the most beautiful creature he had ever seen.

"Allow me to introduce Mademoiselle Jument," croaked Monsieur la Verrue.

"Bonjour, Mademoiselle," said Madame Minette, Monsieur le Canard and Mademoiselle du Merle.

"I, of course, am Monsieur la Verrue. No doubt you have heard of me," continued the toad.

The villagers looked at each other blankly, while in the background Mademoiselle Jument struggled with her suitcase.

"Which one of you fine villagers would like the privilege of having me to stay?" inquired Monsieur la Verrue grandly.

Madame Minette nudged Monsieur Cheval and pointed in the direction of the bus.

"You're the strongest," she whispered. "Quickly, go and help Mademoiselle Jument with her suitcase."

Monsieur Cheval nodded at Madame Minette. "I will!" declared Monsieur Cheval loudly.

Mademoiselle Jument smiled at Monsieur Cheval as he started to make his way towards her.

"Splendid!" said Monsieur la Verrue, who was ignoring the scene behind him. "That's settled, then!"

“No ... I mean ...” said Monsieur Cheval, whirling his head around in confusion. But Monsieur la Verrue had already handed him his suitcase. He looked despondently over the top of Monsieur la Verrue’s warty head and saw that Monsieur Lapin had stepped in to help Mademoiselle Jument. The village baker was helpfully loading her luggage onto his trolley.

“I ... I ...” said Monsieur Cheval in bewilderment.

“I know,” replied Monsieur la Verrue soothingly. “You are worried that your simple rustic abode will not be grand enough for me. But I assure you I am willing to rough it, and it will only be for a week. Come along now. Which way?”

Monsieur Cheval looked to the other villagers for help, but Monsieur le Canard, Mademoiselle du Merle and Madame Minette had suddenly all found something very important to concentrate on between the cobblestones outside the bakery.

"Bother," thought Monsieur Cheval. Not only had he missed an opportunity to help Mademoiselle Jument, he suspected he was probably going to miss out on pastries as well.

4 A Dilapidated Horse

"I observe," said Monsieur la Verrue casually, "that you are rather taken with Mademoiselle Jument." He was unpacking his suitcase, which mostly seemed to be full of toiletries, fancy bow ties and enough mirrors to fill a carnival arcade.

"Yes," said Monsieur Cheval.

"Fortunately, I am somewhat of an expert in these matters," continued Monsieur la Verrue, checking himself in each mirror as it was unpacked. "It is a constant hardship being so attractive and handsome, but one must accept the hand that life has dealt one."

"One must," nodded Monsieur Cheval, wondering what on earth Monsieur la Verrue was talking about.

Monsieur la Verrue looked Monsieur Cheval up and down with a disdainful air and shook his head.

"However, in your case, we may be able to fix it. I'm afraid in your current state of dilapidation and dishevelment, Mademoiselle Jument will not give you a second glance."

Monsieur Cheval looked downcast. Those things, whatever they were, sounded serious.

"But, as they say," said Monsieur la Verrue, "someone, somewhere, is always doing something that someone else said was impossible. I accept the challenge!"

Monsieur Cheval's face brightened.

"Really?" he said.

"We are all obliged to help those less fortunate than ourselves," sighed Monsieur la Verrue wearily. "It is a burden, especially for one as fortunate as me, but I shall shoulder it bravely."

Monsieur Cheval looked at Monsieur la Verrue and, although he couldn't exactly tell the difference between his shoulder and his rotund lumpy neck, and wasn't quite sure where he was going to put the burden, he was relieved by Monsieur la Verrue's generous offer. By the sounds of it, he needed all the help he could get. If he was to have any chance of being friends with Mademoiselle Jument, he needed to be unshevelled and relapidated as soon as possible!

"Now," croaked Monsieur Verrue with a hearty rumble. "What's for lunch?"

"Rrraarp!"

Outside Lapin et fils, the rest of the villagers of Beauchamp had taken up their positions in the sunshine and were enjoying the wafting aroma of fresh pastries baking in Monsieur Lapin's oven.

Monsieur Lapin, who had kindly helped Mademoiselle Jument with her luggage, had offered her a room above the bakery during her stay in Beauchamp, and she had gladly accepted. In return, she suggested that she might help out Monsieur Lapin by serving customers.

"That would be lovely, Mademoiselle," smiled Monsieur Lapin.

"Having to get up every morning at two o'clock means that I am rather tired by the time the bakery opens," he added.

"I'd be happy to help you, Monsieur. I shall start right away," she said.

Mademoiselle Jument found herself an apron and busied herself tidying up the bakery and arranging cake stands, ready to be filled with freshly baked pastries.

Monsieur Lapin went outside and sat on his baker's stool.

"That Mademoiselle Jument is delightful," he said to the other villagers. "I do like her."

"You're not the only one," commented Monsieur le Canard wryly.

"Did you see the way that Monsieur Cheval was looking at her?" winked Madame Minette.

"I knew it the moment he laid eyes upon her," declared Mademoiselle du Merle. "And I'm pretty sure that I heard his heart skip a beat!"

Monsieur Lapin chuckled. His nose twitched and he sniffed the air. The delicious smell of hot pastries was filling the streets of Beauchamp. "I do believe my pastries are ready," he said, stretching and hopping off his stool.

5 A Transformation

Monsieur la Verrue stared at Monsieur Cheval like a sculptor eyeing up a lump of rough marble. He looked this way and that, and Monsieur Cheval bit his tongue nervously.

"Tsk, tsk," muttered Monsieur la Verrue. He frowned and shook his head. "Tsk, tsk."

Monsieur Cheval felt his heart sink. He had had no idea that things were so bad. He had offered to go and fetch some fresh pastries for Monsieur la Verrue's lunch, but the toad had shaken his head vigorously.

"You simply cannot be seen in that state," he said in a horrified tone. "Even though I am starving, what will people think if I let you go out looking like that! As I have now graciously condescended to be your friend, it would reflect badly upon me."

Monsieur Cheval apologised.

"And as for Mademoiselle Jument," said Monsieur la Verrue, sighing heavily, "you can forget about catching her eye."

Monsieur la Verrue set about the task of unshevelling and relapidating Monsieur Cheval with vigour.

"So much to do, so little time," muttered Monsieur la Verrue to himself. Finally, he sat back and looked Monsieur Cheval in the eye.

"We shall start by plucking those ridiculous eyebrows!" he said. "And then we must apply some moustache wax to the fuzz that appears to be growing on your top lip. And then we will fix that dreadful mane with a litre or two of hair cream. And we must get rid of that silly hat and that diabolical shirt."

Monsieur la Verrue's considerable belly rumbled loudly.

"Quickly, Monsieur Cheval!" he said urgently. "If you are to fetch my lunch before I perish from hunger, we do not have a moment to waste!"

The green door of Monsieur Lapin's bakery creaked open and Mademoiselle Jument looked out at Madame Minette, Monsieur le Canard and Mademoiselle du Merle, who were dozing happily in the sun.

"It's lunchtime and Monsieur Lapin's pastries are ready," she said with a smile. "Would anybody like one?"

The villagers shook themselves awake and hungrily lined up inside the bakery. Mademoiselle Jument bustled behind the counter, popping pastries into little brown paper bags and dropping coins into Monsieur Lapin's till.

"Next, please," she said. "Next, please."

Mademoiselle Jument looked up, wondering why the rustling of paper bags and the clinking of coins in pockets had suddenly ceased.

Her eyes widened. Along with the other villagers, she stared at the curious apparition before her.

"Bonjour," purred Monsieur Cheval, stroking his new pencil thin moustache and stylishly cocking the hat that Monsieur la Verrue had generously insisted he borrow. It was hard not to stare at Monsieur Cheval, but harder still not to stare at the glaringly garish shirt he was wearing.

"I ... er ..." stammered Mademoiselle Jument.

Monsieur Cheval raised a strangely curving eyebrow suggestively and tossed his newly lacquered mane nonchalantly. Monsieur la Verrue had assured him that this was a spectacularly successful technique for both romance and shampoo advertisements.

Monsieur Lapin popped his head around the bakery wall to see why everything had suddenly fallen silent. He stared at Monsieur Cheval in disbelief.

"Do you, perchance, have any pastries?" asked Monsieur Cheval.

"Er ... yes, Monsieur, we do," replied Mademoiselle Jument.

"Splendid," said Monsieur Cheval. "If ..."

He momentarily forgot the lines that Monsieur la Verrue had made him recite over and over, and glanced at the small note that he'd pinned to his shirt front just in case.

"Oh, yes," said Monsieur Cheval, finding his place in the scribbled lines. "Ahem. If they are one-tenth as delicious as you, Mademoiselle, I shall take a dozen!"

Mademoiselle Jument, whose face was turning an embarrassed shade of pink, hurriedly found a large brown paper bag and filled it with pastries.

Monsieur Cheval paid for the bag of pastries and whirled around, his head held high. With a backward glance at Mademoiselle Jument, he swept out of the bakery.

Monsieur Lapin, Madame Minette, Mademoiselle du Merle, Monsieur le Canard and Mademoiselle Jument stared at each other. What on earth did Monsieur Cheval think he was doing?

6 Something Is Forgotten

Monsieur la Verrue greedily swallowed his eleventh pastry, flicked his long tongue over his lips, and offered the paper bag to Monsieur Cheval.

"Rrraarp!"

"Would you care to share the last pastry, my good friend?" he asked magnanimously. "I can let you have half."

Monsieur Cheval, who had been surprised to discover just how many pastries could fit in a toad's belly, accepted hungrily.

"I'm not sure that Mademoiselle Jument noticed anything different," he said to Monsieur la Verrue. "She didn't say much."

Monsieur la Verrue burped again.

"You must have patience!" he explained, rolling himself over to get a better view in the mirror. Satisfied, he glanced back at Monsieur Cheval.

"Even the finest artist must wait for the paint to dry before he moves on to the next layers," he said. He sighed and shook his head. "And there is still so much work to do."

"There is?" said Monsieur Cheval, who was examining the bottom of the paper bag for any crumbs that Monsieur la Verrue might have left him.

"Naturally," replied Monsieur la Verrue. "But we must wait until after my nap."

He closed his eyes, rolled over, and let out a huge snore.

Monsieur Cheval scratched his head and settled down to wait.

"I can't imagine what he was thinking," clucked Mademoiselle du Merle. "Monsieur Cheval may be silly, but he's not that silly."

"I've never seen anything like it," mused Monsieur le Canard.

"It's not like Monsieur Cheval at all," said Madame Minette, shaking her head.

Monsieur Lapin swept the last of the crumbs out of his bakery and came and sat on his stool.

"Unfortunately, our friend Monsieur la Verrue seems to be giving him some rather poor advice," said Monsieur Lapin. "Perhaps I should go and have a word."

Monsieur Lapin disappeared down the cobbled laneway towards Monsieur Cheval's stable. But within a couple of minutes, he returned.

"I think he's doing some renovations," he told the villagers. "He wouldn't open the door, but I could hear a noise like a rusty old saw and he kept saying something about waiting for paint to dry."

Monsieur Lapin shrugged.

"I'm sure he'll come to his senses tomorrow," said Madame Minette. "You'll see. When we all wake up for our morning baguette, we'll find the old Monsieur Cheval snoozing in the sunshine outside Lapin et fils, like we always do."

"I hope so," said Monsieur Lapin, wondering if he should bake an extra twelve baguettes just in case.

The next morning, at two o'clock, Monsieur Lapin got up. He walked past the village's stone houses and slipped into his bakery quietly, so as not to wake Mademoiselle Jument who was sleeping upstairs.

For the next four hours, Monsieur Lapin carefully prepared the dough for his long crusty baguettes and when it was ready, he put the bread sticks into the hot stone oven.

As the sun took its first peek above the horizon, Monsieur Lapin placed his hot baguettes in baskets to cool.

Just as he finished, he heard a stirring in the room above and Mademoiselle Jument soon appeared in the doorway.

"Good morning, Monsieur Lapin," she said, yawning.

"Good morning, Mademoiselle Jument," said Monsieur Lapin with a smile. "You are just in time for the best part of a baker's day."

"Really?" said Mademoiselle Jument.

Monsieur Lapin beckoned Mademoiselle Jument outside.

They both sat outside, sniffing the delicious aroma of fresh baguettes drifting out the door.

“Monsieur Lapin,” said Mademoiselle Jument. “I wanted to ask you about that Monsieur Cheval. He seemed quite nice when I first saw him, but now ...” her voice trailed off.

Monsieur Lapin smiled. “He is quite nice,” he said. “But, under the influence of our friend Monsieur la Verrue, he has forgotten something very important.”

"What's that?" asked Mademoiselle Jument.

"Himself," replied Monsieur Lapin simply. "Now," he said, winking, "comes the best part of the day. We watch the sun rise."

7 The Secret

Monsieur Lapin and Mademoiselle Jument snoozed in the warm morning sun as the smell of baguettes twisted and turned its way through the streets of Beauchamp, performing its morning wake-up duties.

Suddenly, Monsieur Lapin felt a nudge. He opened an eye. And then he almost fell off his stool.

“Monsieur Cheval!” he exclaimed. “Is that you?”

“Shh!” whispered Monsieur Cheval. “You’ll wake up Mademoiselle Jument.” He smiled dreamily at the sleeping figure and Monsieur Lapin drew back in alarm.

“What are those?” he said, pointing to Monsieur Cheval’s mouth.

“They are my new false teeth!” replied Monsieur Cheval excitedly.

He flashed Monsieur Lapin a wide smile, showing off two rows of teeth that were far too big for the mouth they were wedged inside. "Do you like them?"

"Well ..." started Monsieur Lapin, before noticing the curious blobs all over Monsieur Cheval's face. "What are those?"

"These are warts!" said Monsieur Cheval. "Well, actually, they're old pieces of newspaper Monsieur la Verrue chewed up and stuck onto my face, but he said they'd do for the time being."

"Really?" said Monsieur Lapin. He noticed Monsieur Cheval's feet. "And what are those?"

"Crocodile skin winklepickers!" beamed Monsieur Cheval. "Do you think Mademoiselle Jument will notice me now?" he whispered anxiously.

Monsieur Lapin looked Monsieur Cheval up and down.

"Yes, my friend, I'm sure she will," he said.

Monsieur Cheval dumped an armful of baguettes on the table and shook Monsieur la Verrue awake.

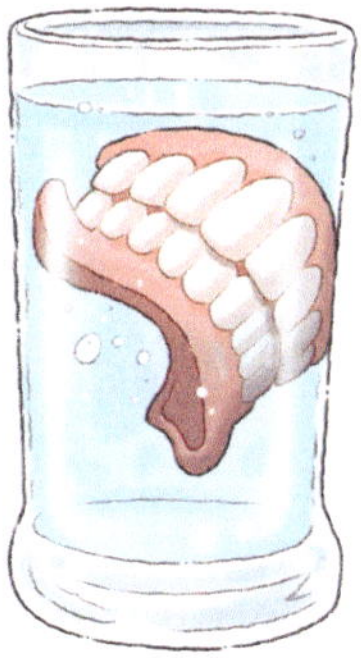

"The paint is still drying," he reported glumly.

"Tsk, tsk," yawned Monsieur la Verrue sleepily. He reached for a baguette. "This will be a long week."

It was a long week. But, to the secret relief of everyone in the village, it did, as they always do, come to an end.

Monsieur Cheval waved sadly as the bus drew away from the Beauchamp arrêt d'autobus. Inside the bus, Monsieur la Verrue gave him a haughty, disdainful, imperious wave, and then admired his reflection in the window and adjusted his bow tie.

Monsieur Cheval turned to the other villagers despondently.

"Now I'll never be good enough for Mademoiselle Jument to notice me," he wailed. "Monsieur la Verrue won't be able to help anymore."

Monsieur Lapin patted his friend on the back.

"You know, as a baker, I have secret ingredients for all my baking," he said mysteriously. "But it's not just baking I have secrets for."

Monsieur Lapin and the villagers smiled at Monsieur Cheval because they felt sorry for him. They knew that his heart was in the right place, even if Monsieur la Verrue had made sure nothing else was.

"Come on, my friend. Mademoiselle Jument will be downstairs soon, so we'd better help you out," said Monsieur Lapin. "I think you might be surprised what she thinks of you if you follow my secret advice."

Monsieur Cheval nodded glumly and Monsieur Lapin disappeared into the bakery. He reappeared with a large rubbish bin.

"Madame Minette, go and collect these things from Monsieur Cheval's barn," instructed Monsieur Lapin, handing her a list.

The other villagers, eager to help their friend, gathered around and listened carefully to Monsieur Lapin's instructions. Soon, the rubbish bin was full of false teeth, the pointy ends of a moustache, crocodile skin winklepickers, stick-on warts, a loud shirt and a ridiculous hat.

Madame Minette hurried back with the hairbrush, towel and the old clothes she'd been sent to get and, very soon, Monsieur Cheval was back to his old dilapidated and dishevelled self.

Monsieur Cheval looked dismayed. The entire week's work had been in vain!

"But ... but ..." he protested.

"Have you guessed by now what the secret is?" winked Monsieur Lapin, sitting on his stool, admiring his handiwork and relaxing in the sunshine.

"The secret?" said Monsieur Cheval.

Monsieur Lapin closed his eyes and enjoyed the warmth of the sunlight on his face.

"Being yourself," he replied simply.

8 A Kiss

"Being myself?" replied Monsieur Cheval. "But I thought that just wasn't good enough. I ..."

Just then, Mademoiselle Jument appeared in the doorway of the bakery. She waved at the villagers and hurried to join them.

Suddenly she noticed Monsieur Cheval, hanging sheepishly behind the others.

"Bonjour, Monsieur Cheval," she said, with a flutter of her eyelashes. "I'm glad to see we have the *real* Monsieur Cheval back with us. He's just like the handsome fellow I saw when I first arrived."

Monsieur Cheval turned beetroot red.

"I didn't like that fellow pretending to be Monsieur Cheval, did you?" she asked the other villagers. Everyone shook their heads vigorously. "He just didn't seem genuine."

And, as she trotted through the group of villagers and past Monsieur Cheval back into the bakery, she blew the startled Monsieur Cheval a kiss.

The villagers giggled, but this time they were giggling with him, not at him. And Monsieur Cheval knew exactly what he had been doing wrong.

He had learnt his lesson:

BEING YOURSELF
ALWAYS MAKES YOU
A BETTER PERSON
THAN TRYING TO BE SOMEONE ELSE.